The White Book

Also by Han Kang

The Vegetarian

Human Acts

HAN KANG
THE WHITE BOOK

TRANSLATED FROM THE KOREAN
BY DEBORAH SMITH

Portobello
Books

Published by Portobello Books in 2017

Portobello Books
12 Addison Avenue
London
W11 4QR

Originally published in Korean in 2016 as 흰
by Munhak Dongne, Seoul.

A CIP catalogue record for this book is
available from the British Library

9 8 7 6 5 4 3 2 1

ISBN 978 1 84627 629 3
eISBN 978 1 84627 630 9

www.portobellobooks.com

Typeset in Athelas by Lindsay Nash

Printed and bound by
CPI Group (UK) Ltd, Croydon, CRO 4YY

The White Book

卜フ

I

I

In the spring, when I decided to write about white things, the first thing I did was to make a list.

Swaddling bands
Newborn gown
Salt
Snow
Ice
Moon
Rice
Waves
Yulan
White bird
'Laughing whitely'
Blank paper
White dog
White hair
Shroud

With each item I wrote down, a ripple of agitation ran through me. I felt that yes, I needed to write this book, and that the process of writing it would be transformative, would itself transform, into something like white ointment applied to a swelling, like gauze laid over a wound. Something I needed.

But then, a few days later, running my eyes over that list again, I wondered what meaning might lie in this task, in peering into the heart of these words.

If I sift those words through myself, sentences will shiver out, like the strange, sad shriek the bow draws from a metal string. Could I let myself hide between these sentences, veiled with white gauze?

This was difficult to answer, so I left the list as it was and put off anything more. I came abroad in August, to this country I'd never visited before, got a short-term lease on a flat in its capital, and learned to draw out my days in these strange environs. One night almost two months later, when the season's chill was just beginning to bite, a migraine set in, viciously familiar. I washed down some pills with warm water, and realised (quite calmly) that hiding would be impossible.

Now and then, the passage of time seems acutely apparent. Physical pain always sharpens the awareness. The migraines that began when I was twelve or thirteen swoop down without warning, bringing with them agonising stomach cramps that stop daily life in its tracks. Even the smallest task is left suspended as I concentrate on simply enduring the pain, sensing time's discrete drops as razor-sharp gemstones, grazing my fingertips. One deep breath drawn in, and this new moment of life takes shape distinct as a bead of blood. Even once I have stepped back into the flow, one day melding seamlessly into another, that sensation remains ever there in that spot, waiting, breath held.

Each moment is a leap forwards from the brink of an invisible cliff, where time's keen edges are constantly renewed. We lift our foot from the solid ground of all our life lived thus far, and take that perilous step out into the empty air. Not because we can claim any particular courage, but because there is no other way. Now, in this moment, I feel that vertiginous thrill course through me. As I step recklessly into time I have not yet lived, into this book I have not yet written.

Door

This was something that happened a long time ago.

Before signing the contract for the lease, I went to look at the flat again.

Its metal door had once been white, but that brightness had faded over time. It was a mess when I saw it, paint flaking off in patches to reveal the rust beneath. And if that had been all, I would have remembered it as nothing more than a scruffy old door. But there was also the way its number, 301, had been inscribed.

Someone – perhaps another in a long line of temporary occupants – had used some sharp implement, maybe a drill bit, to scratch the number into the door's surface. I could make out each individual stroke. 3, itself three hand spans high. 0, smaller, yet gone over several times, a fierce scrawl that attracted attention. Finally, 1, a long, deep-gouged line, taut with the effort of its making. Along this collection of straight and curved wounds rust had spread, a vestige of violence, like long-dried bloodstains, hardened, reddish-black. *I hold nothing dear. Not the place where I live, not the door I pass through every day, not even, damn it, my life.* Those numbers were glaring at me, clenching their teeth tight shut.

That was the flat I wanted that winter, the flat where I'd chosen to spin out my days.

As soon as I'd unpacked, I bought a tin of white paint and a good-sized paintbrush. Neither the kitchen nor the bedroom had been repapered, and their walls were spotted with stains large and small. These dark splotches were especially conspicuous around any electrical switches. I wore pale-grey tracksuit bottoms and an old white sweater, so the splatters wouldn't show up too badly. Even before I'd started to paint, I was unconcerned with achieving a neat, even finish. It would be enough, I reasoned, just to paint over the stains – *surely white splotches are better than dirty ones?* I swept my brush over the large patches on the ceiling where the rain must have seeped through at one time, watching grey disappear beneath white. I gave the sink's grubby bowl a wipe with a flannel before painting it that same bright white, never mind that its pedestal was brown.

Finally, I stepped out into the corridor to paint the front door. With each swish of the brush over the scar-laced surface, its imperfections were erased. Those deep-gouged numbers disappeared, those rusted bloodstains vanished. I went back inside the flat to take a break and get warm, and when I came back out an hour later I saw the paint had run. It looked untidy, probably because I was using a brush rather than a roller. After painting an extra coat over the top so the streaks were less visible, I went back inside to wait. Another hour went by before I shuffled out in my slippers. Snow had begun to scatter down. Outside, the alley had darkened; the street lights were not yet on. Paint tin in one hand, brush in the other, I stood unmoving, a dumb witness to the snowflakes' slow descent, like hundreds of feathers feathering down.

Swaddling bands

Swaddling bands white as snow are wound around the
newborn baby. The womb will have been such a snug
fit, so the nurse binds the body tight, to mitigate the
shock of its abrupt projection into limitlessness.

Person who begins only now to breathe, a first
filling-up of the lungs. Person who does not know who
they are, where they are, what has just begun. The most
helpless of all young animals, more defenceless even
than a newborn chick.

The woman, pale from blood loss, looks at the crying
child. Flustered, she takes its swaddled self into her
arms. Person to whom the cure of this crying is as yet
unknown. Who has been, until mere moments ago,
in the throes of such astonishing agony. Unexpectedly,
the child quiets itself. It will be because of some smell.
Or that the two are still connected. Two black unseeing
eyes are turned towards the woman's face – drawn in
the direction of her voice. Not knowing what has been
set in motion, these two are still connected. In a silence
shot through with the smell of blood. When what lies
between two bodies is the white of swaddling bands.

Newborn gown

My mother's first child died, I was told, less than two hours into life.

I was told that she was a girl, with a face as white as a crescent-moon rice cake. Though she was very small, two months premature, her features were clearly defined. I can never forget, my mother told me, the moment she opened her two black eyes and turned them towards my face.

At the time, my parents were living in an isolated house, in the countryside near the primary school where my father taught. My mother's due date was still far off, so she was completely unprepared when, one morning, her waters broke. There was no one around. The village's sole telephone was in a tiny shop by the bus stop – twenty minutes away. My father wouldn't be back from work for another six hours.

It was early winter, the first frost of the year. My twenty-two-year-old mother crawled into the kitchen and boiled some water to sterilise a pair of scissors. Fumbling in her sewing box, she found some white cloth that would do for a newborn's gown.

Gripped by contractions and terribly afraid, tears started down as she plied her needle. She finished the tiny gown, found a thin quilt to use as swaddling bands, and gritted her teeth as the pain returned, quicker and more intense each time.

Eventually, she gave birth. Still alone, she cut the umbilical cord. She dressed the bloodied little body in the gown she'd just made, and held the whimpering scrap in her arms. For God's sake don't die, she muttered in a thin voice, over and over like a mantra. After an hour had passed, the baby's tight-sealed eyelids abruptly unseamed. As my mother's eyes met those of her child, her lips twitched again. For God's sake don't die. Around an hour later, the baby was dead. They lay there on the kitchen floor, my mother on her side with the dead baby clutched to her chest, feeling the cold gradually enter into the flesh, sinking through to the bone. No more crying.

Moon-shaped rice cake

Last spring, someone asked me whether I'd had
'a particular experience, when you were young, which
brought you close to sadness?' For a radio interview.

Faced with that question, it was this death which
came to me. It was a story which I had grown up inside.
The most helpless of all young animals. Pretty little
baby, white as a moon-shaped rice cake. How I'd been
born and grown up in the place of that death.

'White as a moon-shaped rice cake' never made much
sense until, at six, I was old enough to help out with
making the rice cakes for Chuseok, forming the dough
into small crescent moons. Before being steamed, those
bright white shapes of rice dough are a thing so lovely
they do not seem of this world. Only afterwards, dished
up on a plate with a pine-needle garnish, did they
become disappointingly matter-of-fact. Glistening with
roasted sesame oil, their colour and texture transformed
by heat and steam, they were tasty, of course, but utterly
unlike that former loveliness.

So when my mother said 'white as a rice cake',
I realised, she meant a rice cake before it is steamed.

A face as startlingly pristine as that. These thoughts made my chest grow tight, as though compressed with an iron weight.

Last spring, in the recording studio, I didn't mention any of this. Instead, I spoke of my pet dog, who died when I was five years old. He was an unusually intelligent dog, I said, a mongrel, but descended in part from the famous Jindo breed. I still have a black-and-white photo of the two of us, a candid shot of an intimate moment, but, strangely enough, I cannot remember him alive. My one vivid memory is of the morning when he died. White fur, black eyes, still-damp nose. From then on I developed an aversion to dogs that has persisted to this day. Rather than reaching out to tousle soft fur, my arm stays clamped to my side.

Fog

Why do old memories constantly drift to the surface, here in this unfamiliar city?

When I go out into the streets, the scraps of conversation which pull into focus when the speaker brushes past me, the words stamped on street and shop signs, are almost all incomprehensible. At times my body feels like a prison, a solid, shifting island threading through the crowd. A sealed chamber carrying all the memories of the life I have lived, and the mother tongue from which they are inseparable. The more stubborn the isolation, the more vivid these unlooked-for fragments, the more oppressive their weight. So that it seems the place I flee to is not so much a city on the other side of the world as further into my own interior.

The early hours of the morning, and the city is cloaked in fog.

The border between sky and earth has been scrubbed out. The only view my window offers is the blurred suggestion of two poplars, ink-wash contours wavering four or five metres up from where the street lies hidden;

all else is white. But can we really call it white? That vast, soundless undulation between this world and the next, each cold water molecule formed of drenched black darkness.

I remember a morning on an island long ago, when the fog had been as thick as this. A walk along a cliff path, with the others in the group. Pine trees flickering in and out of existence. Towering ashen cliff. The backs of my companions' heads, which seemed eerily blank and hard-edged as they peered down at the black waters shifting beneath the thick sea fog. But how ordinary a scene that same path showed when I walked it again the following afternoon. What I had fancied a mysterious swamp was a dry, dust-clogged puddle. The pine trees, which had seemed otherworldly when seen in snatched glimpses, were cordoned off by a stretch of barbed wire. The sea's deep blue had the sheen of a tourist postcard. Everything was back within the borders of itself, holding its breath. Holding its breath, and waiting for the next fog.

What do the ghosts of this city do, these muffled early-morning hours?

Slip soundlessly out to walk through the fog that has been holding its breath, and waiting?

Do they greet each other, through the gaps between those water molecules which bleach their voices white?

In some mother tongue of their own, another whose meaning eludes me? Or do they only shake or nod their heads, without the need for words?

White city

I saw some footage of this city, taken by a US military aircraft in the spring of 1945. The film was screened in the projection room on the first floor of the memorial hall, situated in the east of the city. The subtitles said that over a period of six months, starting in October 1944, 95 per cent of the city was obliterated. This city, whose people rose up against the Nazis, from which the German soldiers were driven out in September 1944 and where a month of civilian government was achieved, hence Hitler's decision to use any means necessary to sweep it clean out of existence, as an example.

When the film opened, the city seen from far above appeared as though mantled with snow. A grey-white sheet of snow or ice on which a light dusting of soot had settled, sullying it with dappled stains. The plane reduced its altitude, and the city's visage sharpened. There was no snow covering it, no soot-streaked ice. The buildings had been smashed to pieces, literally pulverised. Above the white glow of stone ruins were blackened flecks as far as the eye could see, showing where the fire had touched.

Riding the bus back to my flat, I got off at the park,
which I'd heard housed a very old castle. After a while
walking through its forested grounds, I came upon
an old hospital building. A faithful reconstruction of
a building that had been destroyed in a 1944 air raid,
no longer used as a hospital but as an art gallery. As I
passed along the narrow trail, vaulted with a mass of
intertwined tree limbs, where the birds' high trill put
me in mind of skylarks, it occurred to me that all of
these things had at one time been dead. These trees
and birds, paths and streets, houses and trams, and all
of these people.

In this city there is nothing that has existed for more
than seventy years. The fortresses of the old quarter,
the splendid palace, the lakeside villa on the outskirts
where royalty once summered – all are fakes. They
are new things, painstakingly reconstructed based on
photographs, pictures, maps. Where a pillar or perhaps
the lower part of a wall happens to have survived, it
has been incorporated into the new structure. The
boundaries which separate old from new, the seams
bearing witness to destruction, lie conspicuously
exposed.

It was on that day, as I walked through the park, that
she first came into my mind.

A person who had met the same fate as that city. Who had at one time died or been destroyed. Who had painstakingly rebuilt themselves on a foundation of fire-scoured ruins. Who was therefore something new. Who, some broken pediment having survived, has ended up bearing a strange pattern, the new distinct from the old.

Certain objects in the darkness

Certain objects appear white in the darkness.

When darkness is imbued with even the faintest light, even things which would not otherwise be white glow with a hazy pallor.

At night, I make up the sofa bed in the corner of the living room and lie down in that wan light. Instead of trying to sleep, I wait, feel my senses attune to the passage of time. The trees outside the window cast silhouettes onto the white plaster wall. I think about the person who resembles this city, pondering the cast of their face. Waiting for its contours to coalesce, to be able to read the expression it holds.

The direction of the light

I read an account by a man born in this city, in which he
claimed to have lived for as long as he could remember
with the soul of his elder brother, who had died aged
six in the Jewish ghetto. The child's voice came to
him from time to time, he said, with neither form nor
texture. In addition, the language was foreign to him,
as he'd been adopted by a Belgian couple and grown
up in that country, meaning he hadn't at first been able
to tell that the speaker was his brother. It could only
be a waking dream, he thought, in which everything is
doomed to recur, or else a symptom of derangement.
When, at the age of eighteen, he finally came to learn
of his family history, he began to study the language of
this country, to understand what this soul was trying to
tell him. And thus he learned of his brother's fear, this
brother both older and younger. That he was screaming
the same handful of terror-struck words, choked out
when the soldiers had come to arrest him.

I slept badly for several days after reading this, unable
to stop my thoughts from turning to the final moments

of that six-year-old child, who would ultimately have been murdered. In the small hours of one such restless night, when the roiling inside me had finally calmed, it occurred to me that if I had been similarly visited myself, by my mother's first child who had lived just two hours, I would have been utterly oblivious. Because the girl had never learned language at all. For an hour she had held her eyes open, held them in the direction of our mother's face, but her optic nerves never had time to awaken, and so that face had remained beyond reach. For her, there would have been only a voice. *Don't die. For God's sake don't die.* Unintelligible words, the only words she was ever to hear.

And so I can neither confirm nor deny that there are times when she has sought me out, hovering at my forehead or by the corners of my eyes. That some vague sensation I had known as a child, some stirring of seemingly unprompted emotion, might, unbeknown to me, have been coming from her. For there are moments, lying in the darkened room, when the chill in the air is a palpable presence. *Don't die. For God's sake don't die.* Turned towards indecipherable sounds laden with love and anguish. Towards a pale blur and body heat. Perhaps I too have opened my eyes in the darkness, as she did, and gazed out.

Breast milk

The twenty-two-year-old woman lies alone in the
house. Saturday morning, with the first frost still
clinging to the grass, her twenty-five-year-old husband
goes up the mountain with a spade to bury the baby
who was born yesterday. The woman's puffy eyes will
not open properly. The various hinges of her body
ache, swollen knuckles smart. And then, for the first
time, she feels warmth flood into her chest. She sits up,
clumsily squeezes her breast. First a watery, yellowish
trickle, then smooth white milk.

She

I think of her living to drink that milk.

I think of stubborn breathing, of tiny lips mumbling at the nipple.

I think of her being weaned and then raised on rice porridge, growing up, becoming a woman, making it through every crisis.

I think of death deflected every time, faced with her back as she moves firmly forwards.

Don't die. For God's sake don't die.

Because of those words knitted into her, an amulet in her body.

And I think of her coming here instead of me.

To this curiously familiar city, whose death and life resemble her own.

Candle

As I have imagined her, she walks this city's streets.
At a crossroads, she sees a section of red brick wall.
In the process of reconstructing yet another shattered
building, the wall had been taken down and rebuilt a
metre in front of its original position, along with a low
epitaph explaining that the German army used it to line
up civilians and shoot them. Someone has put a vase
of flowers in front of it, and several white candles are
crowned with wavering flames.

Wreaths of fog still shroud the city, less thick than
in the early morning, translucent as tracing paper.
If a strong wind got up and skimmed off the fog,
the ruins of seventy years ago might be startled into
revealing themselves, pushing out from behind the
present reconstructions. The ghosts that were gathered
there, very close to her, might stand up straight against
the wall where they were slaughtered, their eyes
blazing out.

But there is no wind, and nothing is revealed beyond
the already apparent. The warm white candle wax
creeps ever downwards. Feeding themselves to the

white wicks' flames, these stubs sink steadily lower,
eventually out of existence.

Now I will give you white things,

What is white, though may yet be sullied;
Only white things will I give.

No longer will I question

Whether I should give this life to you.

2

She

그
녀

Rime

The window not quite flush in its frame, allowing rime to form on its glass. Midwinter. That pattern of frozen white recalled the snow ice that forms on a stream's surface. The writer Park T'ae-won said that just such a window had drawn his gaze when his first daughter was born, hence the name he coined for her: Seol-yeong. Snow flower.

She'd once seen the sea itself frozen over. An unusually shallow stretch of water, compounded by a cold current, had formed serried ranks of frozen waves, like layer upon layer of dazzling white flowers captured in the moment of unfurling. She saw frozen fish strewn over the sandy shore, the hard glint of their scales. On such days, the people of that region say 'the sea is rimed over'.

Frost

The day she was born was one of frost rather than
snow, yet her father chose *seol*, snow, as one of the
characters for his daughter's name. Growing up,
she was unusually sensitive to the cold, and resented
the chill embedded in her name.

But she liked to tread the frost-covered ground and
feel the semi-frozen earth through the soles of her
trainers. The first frost, as yet untrodden, has the fine
crystals of pure salt. The sun's rays pale slightly as the
frost begins to form. White clouds of breath bloom
from warm mouths. Trees shiver off their leaves,
incrementally lightening their burden. Solid objects
like stones or buildings appear subtly more dense.
Seen from behind, men and women bundled up in
heavy coats are saturated with a mute presentiment,
that of people beginning to endure.

Wings

It was on the outskirts of this city that she saw the
butterfly. A single white butterfly, wings folded on a
reed bed, one November morning. No butterflies had
been seen since summer; where could this one have
been hiding? The air temperature had plummeted
in the previous week, and it was perhaps on account
of its wings frequently freezing that the white colour
had leached from them, leaving certain parts close
to transparent. So clear, they shimmer with the black
earth's reflection. Only a little time is needed now, and
the whiteness will leave those wings completely. They
will become something other, no longer wings, and the
butterfly will be something that is no longer butterfly.

Fist

Walking this city's streets until her calves had grown stiff, she waited. For something of her native language, sentences or even mere scraps of words, to surge swiftly to the tip of her tongue. She thought she might be able to write about snow. In this city, where they say it snows for half the year.

She kept a dogged watch for the coming of winter. Studied the shop windows, the reflections shown there not yet blurred by streaks of snow. The heads of others passing through the streets, still with no powdery dusting. Those slanting forms, not yet snowflakes, barely grazing the foreheads of strangers. Her own cold fists, which she clenched to white.

Snow

Against the background of a black coat sleeve, a large flake of snow will reveal its crystals even to the naked eye. A scant couple of seconds and she has witnessed it all. Mysterious hexagons melting clean away.

When it first begins to fall, people stop what they are doing and turn their attention to the snow. On a bus, they lift their eyes from their laps and gaze out of the window for a time. Once the snow has been soundlessly strewn about, with an equal absence of joy or sorrow, and the street's erasure is complete, the people turn their faces away, and the blurring streaks are no longer reflected in their eyes.

Snowflakes

One late night long ago, she'd seen a man lying at
the foot of a telegraph pole. He was slumped on his
side. Had he fallen? Was he drunk? Should she call an
ambulance? While she vacillated, unable to move away
from the scene yet wary of drawing nearer, the man
heaved himself half up and focused his blank gaze on
her. She flinched, startled; though there seemed no
immediate threat of violence, the alley was otherwise
deserted. She walked on with hurried steps, then
turned to look back. The man was squatting on the cold
pavement, still in the same awkward position, staring
piercingly at the grimy rendered wall which stretched
along the alley's opposite side.

he who had shipwrecked himself in an alley, who
   had pushed himself up on cold-numbed hands,
thinking of what his life has been,
of the loneliness that waits for him at home,
thinking what is this, what the hell is this
damned dirty white

falling snow.

*

Sparse flakes fly in all directions.
In the black air where the street lights do not touch.
Whirled above the black branches of wordless trees.
Brushing against the bowed heads trudging through
the night.

Perpetual snow

She'd considered living somewhere in sight of
perpetual snow. Where the bodies of trees clustered
close outside her window would mark each shift in
season against the unchanging backdrop, off in the
distance, of permanently ice-capped mountains.
Cool as the hands on her fevered forehead when she
lay at home on a school day.

There was a black-and-white film made here in
1980, in which the protagonist lost his father when
he was seven years old, and was raised by his calm,
gentle mother. (His father had been only twenty-nine
when he met with disaster, climbing the Himalayas
with a group of friends. His body was never found.)
The son moved out of his mother's house as soon as
he was old enough, and lived by an incredibly strict
code of ethics. Whenever he had to make a decision,
he would see in his mind's eye an oppressive landscape:
fresh snow falling on the icebound Himalayas, like
a whiteout inside his head. Each time, he made the
choice that went hardest with himself, the choice which
many others would have quailed at. In a period when

corruption was rife, he alone refused to take bribes, and for that he was ostracised, even physically attacked. In the end, he walked into a trap, was hounded out of his place of work and returned home alone. There, allowing himself to become lost in thought, the peaks and ravines of that far mountain range filled up his field of vision. The very place where he could not go. The land of ice, in which his father's frozen body was hidden, where humans were not suffered to tread.

Wave

In the distance, the surface of the water bulges upwards. The winter sea mounts its approach, surging closer in. The wave reaches its greatest possible height and shatters in a spray of white. The shattered water slides back over the sandy shore.

Standing at this border where land and water meet, watching the seemingly endless recurrence of the waves (though this eternity is in fact illusion: the earth will one day vanish, everything will one day vanish), the fact that our lives are no more than brief instants is felt with unequivocal clarity.

Each wave becomes dazzlingly white at the moment of its shattering. Further out, the tranquil body of water flashes like the scales of innumerable fish. The glittering of multitudes is there. The shifting, stirring, tossing of multitudes. Nothing is eternal.

Sleet

There is none of us whom life regards with any partiality. Sleet falls as she walks these streets, holding this knowledge inside her. Sleet that leaves cheeks and eyebrows heavy with moisture. Everything passes. She bears this remembrance – the knowledge that everything she has clung to will fall away from her and vanish – through the streets where the sleet is falling, that is neither rain nor snow, neither ice nor water, that dampens her eyebrows and streams from her forehead whether she stands still or hurries on, closes her eyes or opens them.

White dog

What's a dog that's a dog, but doesn't bark?

She was a child when she first heard this riddle. When, or from whom, she doesn't remember now.

The summer when she was twenty-four, when she'd quit her first job and gone back to the house she'd grown up in, she saw a white dog in the neighbours' yard. Previously, this had been the home of a vicious Tosa, originally bred as a fighting dog. It used to rush forwards, stretching the rope as taut as it would go, and snap its jaws. All it needed was for the rope around its neck to be loosened or snap for it to fly at you and sink its teeth into your flesh. Though she knew the dog was tied up, she still kept as far away from it as possible whenever she had to pass the gate, intimidated by its viciousness.

Chained up now in that Tosa's place was a mongrel with perhaps a faint strain of Jindo blood. Its body was dotted with patches of bare flesh, pale pink coins amid the dull white of its fur. This dog neither barked nor even growled. When it first met her eye it drew back, startled, the chain around its neck rasping over the cement floor. It was August, and the scorching sun was unrelenting. Perhaps because of the muggy heat, the road through the village was deserted. The silence was broken only by the chain's harsh grating each time the dog flinched back. At her slightest movement it startled afresh, pressed itself even further to the ground and scrabbled back, dragging the chain over the floor. Keeping its eyes fixed on her the whole time. Terror. It was terror that she read in those two black eyes.

That evening she asked about the dog. 'It doesn't even bark if it sees a stranger,' her mother said, 'just cowers and trembles, so the owner's thinking of selling it on again. What if a burglar came?'

The dog never lost its fear of her. Even on her last day at home, when it had had a full week to become used to her, it cringed close to the ground and jerked backwards as soon as she appeared outside the gate. It twisted its head against its flank as though something was pressing against its windpipe. Though its tongue lolled out between its teeth, there was no audible panting. The only sound the dog could be said to produce was the low rasp of the chain against the cement. Even the sight of her mother, a familiar face of several months' acquaintance, would provoke this same startled reaction. *Okay now, it's okay.* Her voice was soft and soothing as she walked unhurriedly on.

Poor wretch, she muttered, clicking her tongue, *it must have suffered a lot.*

A dog that's a dog, but doesn't bark?

The lacklustre answer to the riddle is fog.

And so for her, the dog's name became Fog. A large white dog that doesn't bark. A dog that bore a physical resemblance to her childhood pet, now a hazy memory from the distant past.

That winter when she went down again to her family home, there was no Fog. Instead, she was greeted by a squat brown bulldog that snarled with great gusto.

What happened to that other dog?

Her mother shook her head.

The owner had it up for sale the whole summer, but he couldn't quite bring himself to part from it; then when the frost came and the temperature suddenly dropped, it died. It got sick and stopped touching its food, just lay there on its front… and the whole time, it didn't make a single sound.

Blizzard

A few years ago there was a heavy-snow warning. Seoul
was in the grip of a blizzard as she walked alone on a hill
path. Her umbrella proved next to useless at keeping the
snow off. She carried on walking, white flakes whirling
thick and fast around her face and body. Unable to
fathom what on earth it could be, this thing so cold, so
hostile. This vanishing fragility, this oppressive weight
of beauty.

Ashes

That winter, she and her younger brother made a
six-hour drive to a beach on the south coast. The box
holding their mother's powdered bones they enshrined
in an ossuary; the small temple nearby with a view of
the distant sea would house the woman's soul. The
monks would chant her name with their sutras in the
early hours of each morning. On Buddha's birthday
a paper lantern would be lit in her memory.

With those voices, those lights near at hand, our
mother's ashes would lie in changeless calm inside
a sealed stone drawer.

Salt

One day she took a handful of coarse salt and examined it closely. Those crystals had a cool beauty, their white touched with grey. For the first time, she had a real sense of the power that lay within this material: the power to preserve, the power to sterilise and to heal.

There had been a time before that when she was preparing food and picked up salt with an injured hand. If letting the knife slip was the first mistake, made because she was pressed for time, allowing salt to touch the unbandaged cut was the second, and worst. That was when she'd learned how it actually felt, the expression 'to pour salt on a wound'.

Some time later, she saw a photograph of an installation in which a hill of salt had been constructed, on which visitors were then invited to rest their bare feet. After sitting on the chair that had been put there for that purpose and removing your shoes and socks, you put both feet up on the salt and could sit like that for as long as you wanted. The photograph showed a dark exhibition space, with the only spot of trembling light being the summit of the salt hill, which was a little taller than the height of a person. The exhibition visitor, whose face was in shadow, sat on the chair with her bare feet resting on the slope of salt. Perhaps because she had been like that for a long time, the white salt hill and the woman's body appeared to have fused together, naturally and painfully.

To do that, she thought, studying the photograph, *you'd have to have feet with no wounds or scars. Only if my feet were fully healed could I rest them on that mountain of salt. Where the shade retains a certain chill, however white it shines.*

Moon

When clouds swim in front of the moon and obscure
its light completely, those same clouds instantly shine
white and cold. When black clouds are mixed in with
the white, a delicate chiaroscuro is formed. Behind that
pattern of dappling dark, the wan moon is concealed,
wreathed with ashen or lilac or pale blue light, full
or halved or a shape more slender still, waning to a
single sliver.

Each time she gazed up at the mid-month moon she
would see a person's face. Ever since she was very young,
all the grown-ups' explanations had fallen on deaf ears:
she never could manage to make out the shapes she
was told were there, the pair of rabbits and the mortar
they pound rice in. All that was apparent were two
eyes, seemingly lost in thought, above the shadowed
suggestion of a nose.

On nights when the moon is unusually large, she
can leave the curtains open and let its light flood every
inch of her flat. She can pace, then, up and down. In the
light filtering out of a huge white pondering face, the
darkness soaking out of two black eyes.

Lace curtain

Is it because of some billowing whiteness within us,
unsullied, inviolate, that our encounters with objects
so pristine never fail to leave us moved? Her passage
through the frozen streets brings her to the building,
where her gaze lifts to the first floor. To the flimsy lace
curtain hanging there.

There are times when the crisp white of freshly
laundered bed linen can seem to speak. When that
pure-cotton fabric grazes her bare flesh, just there,
it seems to tell her something. You are a noble person.
Your sleep is clean, and the fact of your living is nothing
to be ashamed of. Such is the strange comfort she
receives, at that in-between time when sleep borders
wakefulness, when that crisp cotton bedsheet brushes
her skin.

Breath-cloud

On cold mornings, that first white cloud of escaping
breath is proof that we are living. Proof of our bodies'
warmth. Cold air rushes into dark lungs, soaks up the
heat of our body and is exhaled as perceptible form,
white flecked with grey. Our lives' miraculous diffusion,
out into the empty air.

White birds

A congregation of white gulls on the winter shore.
Around twenty, perhaps? The birds were sitting facing
out to sea, where the sun was creeping down to the
horizon. As though observing some kind of silent
ceremony, holding themselves perfectly still in the
sub zero cold as they witnessed the day's decline.
She stopped walking and let her gaze follow theirs,
to that pallid source of light which was about to flush
crimson. Though the cold was so severe it seemed to
sink its teeth right down to her bones, it was precisely
the heat from that light, she knew, that kept her body
from freezing.

A crane by the water's edge, one Seoul summer's day.
Entirely white save for its bright-red feet. The bird was
picking his way out of the water and up onto a smooth,
broad rock. Was he aware of her gaze? Perhaps. And
also that she meant him no harm? Hence his impassive
expression as he faced the opposite bank, letting the
sun's rays dry his red feet.

*

Why do white birds move her in a way that other birds do not? She doesn't know. Why do they seem so especially graceful, at times almost sacred? Now and then, she dreams of a white bird flying away. In the dream, the white bird is very close, so close it seems she could reach out and grasp it as it flies forwards, beating its wings in utter silence, the sunlight slanting off its feathers. It flies far away, and yet, somehow, never beyond the reach of her gaze. Gliding through the air, eternally unvanishing. Its dazzling wings fanned out from its sides.

What should she make of it, the white bird alighting briefly on her head and then flying off again, here in this city? She'd been on her way home, fretting about something, trudging through the park and along the stream's bank. Something swooped down and settled its huge self on the crown of her head. After extending both wings so that they enveloped the sides of her face like a wimple, the tips of its feathers almost brushing her cheeks, it lifted away and flew to the roof of a nearby building, as though it had had no business with her at all.

Handkerchief

She saw it one afternoon in late summer, as she was
walking past a secluded tenement building. A woman
on the second floor was hanging her washing out
over the balcony rail when a handful of items slipped
from her grasp. A single handkerchief drifted down,
slowest of all, finally to the ground. Like a bird with its
wings half furled. Like a soul tentatively sounding out
a place it might alight.

Milky Way

Once winter set in, almost every day in this city was
overcast, and she could no longer see the stars in the
night sky. The air temperature dropped below zero,
and a pattern began in which days of continuous rain
alternated with days of snow. The low air pressure gave
her frequent headaches. The birds hugged the ground
as they flew. The sun began to set at around three
o'clock in the afternoon, and by four it was utterly dark.

Raising her eyes to the afternoon sky as she walked,
a black that her homeland knew only at night, her mind
turned to thoughts of nebulae. To the thousands of
stars like grains of salt whose light had streamed down
to her, those nights at her parents' countryside home.
Clean, cold light that had bathed her eyes, scouring her
mind of all memory.

Laughing whitely

The expression 'laughing whitely' (probably) exists
only in her mother tongue. Laughter that is faint,
cheerless, its cleanness easily shattered. And the face
that forms it.

'You laughed whitely, you know.'
    In this instance, 'you' would (probably) be someone
who managed to force a laugh, quietly enduring some
internal struggle.

'He laughed whitely.'
    Here, 'he' would (probably) be someone struggling to
part from something inside himself.

Yulan

Two of her university classmates died in relatively
swift succession, one at the age of twenty-four and one
at twenty-three. The former in a bus crash, the latter
during his military service. A few months after this
second accident, in early spring, former students from
the same graduating class clubbed together to purchase
two yulan saplings, which they planted on the hill
in the university grounds, overlooking the classroom
where the two students had studied literature together.

Some years later, walking beneath those flowing
trees, which spoke of life – rejuvenation, revivification –
she wondered: what made us choose yulan? Because
white flowers have to do with life? Or with death? She'd
read somewhere that the words 'blank' and *'blanc'*,
'black' and even 'flame', literally 'fire flower' in Korean,
all have the same root in Indo-European languages.
Blank white flowers of fire, blazing in the surrounding
dark – the brief March blooming of two yulans.

Small white pills

Now and then she finds herself wondering, and not out
of self-pity, but with a detached, almost idle curiosity:
if you could add up all the pills she'd ever taken, what
would the total be? How many hours of pain has she
lived through? As though life itself wished to impede
her progress, she was brought up short again and
again. As though the force which prevents her moving
forwards to the light stands always at the ready inside
her own body. All those hours when she had lost
her way, in hesitation and in doubt. How many would
there be? How many small white pills?

Sugar cubes

She was around ten years old at the time. Her first outing to a coffee shop, accompanied by her aunt, was also the first time she set eyes on sugar cubes. Those squares wrapped in white paper possessed an almost unerring perfection, surely too perfect for her. She peeled the paper carefully off and brushed a finger over that granular surface. She crumbled a corner, touched it to her tongue, nibbled at that dizzying sweetness, then eventually placed it in a cup of water and sighed as she watched it melt away.

She isn't really partial to sweet things any more, but the sight of a dish of wrapped sugar cubes still evokes the sense of witnessing something precious. There are certain memories which remain inviolate to the ravages of time. And to those of suffering. It is not true that everything is coloured by time and suffering. It is not true that they bring everything to ruin.

Lights

In this city of severe winters, a December night
unspools itself around her. The darkness outside
the window has no moon to soften it. In the small
workshop to the rear of the building, presumably
as a security measure, a dozen electric lights are left
on all through the night. She looks at the patches of
illumination, scattered and isolated amid the black.
Since she came to this place, or no, in fact before, her
sleep has been scattered and shallow. Even if she did
drop off for a while, she would rise to find the world
just as dark as before. If, by some stroke of luck, she
were able to manage a longer sleep, the blue tinge of
a sluggish dawn would be seeping steadily from within
the black. Yet those lights will be frozen white as ever,
in the clarity of their stillness, in their isolation.

A thousand points of silver

On such a night, without the slightest reason, the sea
surges up.

The boat is so small that even the slightest wave
sends it pitching and yawing violently. Eight years old
and afraid, she crouches in the bottom of the boat,
shoulders hunched. At just such a moment, a thousand
points of silver sweep in from the distant sea and pass
beneath the hull. In an instant she forgets her fear,
gazing wide-eyed after the turbulent motion of that
glittering immensity.

    An anchovy shoal, her uncle laughs. He had been
sitting at the stern the whole time, barely batting an
eyelid. A tangled mop of curly hair above a swarthy
face. He never did see forty: his addiction to alcohol
would carry him away in the space of two years.

Glittering

What is it about minerals that glimmer, like silver,
gold or diamonds, that makes people think of them
as noble? One theory puts it down to the fact that,
for early man, the glittering of water signalled life.
Shining water meant clean water. Only water that is
drinkable – that gives life – is transparent. Whenever,
after trekking through deserts, forests and foetid
swamps, a group was able to discern a body of water
glittering white in the distance, they would have felt
lacerated by happiness. Which would have been life.
Which would have been beauty.

White pebble

A long time ago she found a white pebble on a beach.
She brushed off the sand and placed it in her pocket,
then put it away in a drawer at home. A pebble worn
smooth and round by the waves' long caress. To her,
its whiteness seemed almost transparent, but when she
tried to peer inside it she found she'd been mistaken.
(In fact, it was a perfectly ordinary white pebble.) Now
and then she got it out and sat it on her palm. If silence
could be condensed into the smallest, most solid object,
this is how it would feel, she thought.

White bone

She was once X-rayed to try to determine the cause
of the pain which afflicted her. The skeleton in the
Röntgen image, grey-white bones in a gunmetal
sea. It startled her to see it like that: something with
the solid materiality of stone, steadfast inside the
human body.

A long time before that, around puberty, she had
become fascinated by the names of the various
bones. Anklebone and kneebone. Collarbone and
rib. Breastbone and crossbar bone, another name for
collarbone. That human beings are also constructed
of something other than flesh and muscle seemed
to her like a strange stroke of luck.

Sand

And she frequently forgot,
That her body (all our bodies) is a house of sand.
That it had shattered and is shattering still.
Slipping stubbornly through fingers.

White hair

She remembers one of her bosses, a middle-aged man who used to say how he longed to see a former lover again in old age, when her hair would be feather-white. *When we're really old… when every single strand of our hair has gone white, I want to see her then, absolutely.*

If there was a time when he would want to see her again, it would certainly be then.

When both youth and flesh would have fallen away.

When there would be no time left for desire.

When only one thing would remain to be done once that meeting was over: to separate. To part from their own bodies, and thus to part forever.

Clouds

That summer, we saw the clouds passing over the
fields while we were sitting out in front of Unju temple,
remember? Huddled together, gazing at the Buddha that
had been carved into the rock's flat surface. Shadows of huge
clouds slid swiftly by, side by side between land and sky.

Incandescent bulb

Her desk has been swept bare. There is only the incandescent bulb above it, giving off light and heat.

All is still.

The blind has not been lowered, and headlights can be seen moving along the main road at sporadic intervals now that midnight has passed.

She is sitting at the desk, like someone who has never known suffering.

Not like someone who has just been crying, or is about to.

Like someone who has never shattered.

As though there has never been a time when the only comfort lay in the impossibility of forever.

White nights

She learned of its existence after coming to this city:
an inhabited island at the northernmost point of
Norway, where the summer sun hangs in the sky the
whole day, while in winter those twenty-four hours
are all night. She wondered what daily life would
be like in such an extreme environment. Is the time
being measured out around her now another such
white night, or is it a black day? Stale pain has not yet
withered quite away, fresh pain has not yet burst into
bloom. Days in which darkness and light are both
imperfect swell with memories of the past. The only
things which the mind cannot examine are memories
of the future. Ahead of her now is an amorphous light,
flickering like some gas of unknown composition.

Island of light

The moment she went up on stage, the ceiling spotlight
flicked on, its strong beam picking her out. At that,
all space that was not the stage became a sea of black.
That an audience was sitting there seemed wholly
unreal, and she was thrown into confusion. Do I
go down into that ocean floor, step by faltering step,
or stand my ground here in this island of light?

Black writing through white paper

Each time she groped her way back to health, she
would find that life now cast a certain chill. A feeling
which it would be too feeble to call 'resentment',
too severe to call 'rancour'. As though the one who
had been tucking her in and kissing her forehead each
night had suddenly turned on her yet again, driving
her out of the house into the cold, making her painfully
aware that all those sunny smiles had been only on
the surface.

Looking at herself in the mirror, she never forgot
that death was hovering behind that face. Faint yet
tenacious, like black writing bleeding through thin
paper.

    Learning to love life again is a long and complicated
process.

    Because at some point you will inevitably cast me
      aside.
    When I am at my weakest, when I am most in need
      of help,

You will turn your back on me, cold and irrevocable.
And that is something perfectly clear to me.
And I cannot now return to the time before that
knowledge.

Scattering

Before the day drew to a close, slushy snow began to fall.

In the blink of an eye, the ash-grey streets of the old town were erased into whiteness. A whiteness that seemed too perfect to be real, showing up the shabby figures that moved against its canvas, their threadbare cloaks of ordinary hours. Like them, she walked without stopping. Through beauty that would disappear – was disappearing already. Mutely.

To the stillness

When the day of her leaving draws near,
and she stands in the darkness of this house, there
    are words she will want to speak to its stillness,
    which she is no longer permitted to dwell inside.
When the night that had seemed without end is over
    and the northeastern window is a swatch of deep-
    blue twilight,
when the sky then brightens to ultramarine and the
    clean bones of poplars are slowly outlined,
there will be something she wants to say to the
    stillness, in the early hours of Sunday morning
    when the building's other inhabitants have yet
    to stir.

Please, a little longer like this.

To give it time to wash me clean.

Boundary

She grew up inside this story.

She was born prematurely, at seven months. Her twenty-two-year old mother was entirely unprepared when the contractions came. The first frost of the year was early. Her mother was alone in the house. The baby cried only briefly after coming into the world, a thin, wavering sound that soon petered out. Her mother dressed the small, bloodied body in a baby gown and wrapped her carefully in a padded quilt, making sure not to smother her. At first, when the baby fastened to the empty breast, instinct produced a feeble sucking, but this too soon subsided. The baby was laid gently down on the warmest part of the heated floor, but by this point she was no longer crying, her eyes were no longer open. Now and then her mother would be struck by a sense of foreboding and give a corner of the quilt a tug, but the baby's eyes opened only briefly, grew dim and then slid shut. At some point, even that scant response was no longer forthcoming. And yet, before dawn, when the first milk finally came from her mother's breasts and she pressed her nipple between the tiny lips, she found that, despite everything, the baby was still breathing. Though she had, by now, slipped from consciousness, the nipple in her mouth encouraged a soft swallowing, gradually growing stronger. Still with her eyes closed the whole time. Not knowing what boundary she was now passing over.

Reedbed

One morning after a night of snow, she walks into
a reedbed. She parts the reeds, each slender white
stalk bent under the weight of the snow. The reedbed
surrounds a small marsh, where a pair of wild ducks are
living. At its heart, where the thin sheet of ice meets still
water, the ducks float side by side on its greyish-blue
surface, necks bowed to drink.

Before turning back from them, she asks herself: do you
want to go on? To push forwards? Is it worth it?

There was a time when she had answered, trembling, no.
   Now she walks, holding any answer in reserve. She
leaves that semi-frozen marsh, between dreariness and
delicacy.

White butterfly

Were it not the case that life stretches out in a straight
line, she might at some point become aware of having
rounded a bend. Bringing, perhaps, the realisation that
nothing of that past could now be glimpsed were she to
cast a quick glance over her shoulder. This road might
be covered not with snow or frost but with the soft
tenacity of pale-green spring grasses. A white butterfly
stuttering forwards might snatch at her gaze, tug her
a few paces further in the wake of those wingbeats,
like a soul's fretful palpitations. She might become
aware only then of the surrounding trees, their slow
reanimation as though in thrall to something, giving off
a strange and stifling scent, flaring up into a still more
lush proliferation, into thin air, towards the light.

Spirit

Were spirits to exist, she thought, their motion would be the invisible correlate of just such a butterfly's trembling flight.

If that were so, would the souls of this city sometimes drift to the wall where they were once gunned down, and flutter there for a time with such a soundless motion? But she knew that the people of this city did not light candles and lay flowers in front of that wall only for the sake of such souls. They believe that there is no shame in having been butchered. They want to draw out their grief for as long as possible.

She thought of certain incidents in her own country's history, the country she had left in order to come here, of the dead that had been insufficiently mourned. Trying to imagine those souls being thus eulogised, in the very heart of the city streets, she realised that her country had never once done this properly.

And, less significantly, she learned what had been left out of her own reconstruction. Of course, her body had not yet died. Her spirit still had flesh to house it. Like the remaining section of a ruined brick wall, which the bombing had not managed to destroy completely, since moved and incorporated into another structure – from which the blood has been washed clean. Flesh which was now no longer young.

As she walked she imitated the steady gait of one who had never been broken. A clean cloth veiling each unstitched place. Doing without farewells, without mourning. If she believes that she has never been shattered, she can believe that she will be shattered no more.

And so, there are a few things left to her:

To stop lying.

To (open her eyes and) remove the veil.

To light a candle for all the deaths and spirits she can remember – including her own.

Rice raw and cooked

She walks in search of rice to cook for dinner. Finding
sticky rice in this city is easier said than done. Even in
a large supermarket the closest she gets is some Spanish
rice, sold in small plastic packs of five hundred grams.
The white grains lie quiet in her bag as she carries them
home. White steam rises from the bowl of just-cooked
rice, and she sits in front of it as though at prayer. She
cannot deny that, at that moment, she feels something
inside her. To deny it is impossible.

3

All Whiteness

온

통

흰

The year after she lost her first child, she had another premature birth. I was told that the baby, a boy this time, managed even fewer months in the womb than the girl had, and died soon after being born, without once opening his eyes. Had those lives made it safely past the point of crisis, my own birth which followed three years later, and that of my brother four years after that, would not have come about. My mother would not have lived with those shattered memories inside her, running her fingers carefully over their sharp edges.

This life needed only one of us to live it. If you had lived beyond those first few hours, I would not be living now.

My life means yours is impossible.

Only in the gap between darkness and light, only in that blue-tinged breach, do we manage to make out each other's faces.

Your eyes

I saw differently when I looked with your eyes. I walked
differently when I walked with your body. I wanted
to show you clean things. Before brutality, sadness,
despair, filth, pain, clean things that were only for
you, clean things above all. But it didn't come off as
I intended. Again and again I peered into your eyes,
as though searching for form in a deep, black mirror.

If only we'd been living in a city back then, I heard
my mother say several times during my childhood.
If only an ambulance could have taken me to hospital.
If only they'd put her in an incubator, that tiny rice cake
of a baby. They were a new thing then, incubators.

If only you hadn't stopped breathing. And had
therefore been granted all this life in my stead, I who
would then never have been born. If it had been
granted to you to go firmly forwards, with your own
eyes and your own body, your back to that dark mirror.

Shroud

What did you do with her, with the baby?

The night I first asked my father this, when I was almost out of my teens and he was not yet fifty, he was silent for a while before answering.

Wrapped her in a white shroud, took her to the mountain and buried her.

Alone?

That's right. Alone.

The girl's baby gown became a shroud. Her swaddling bands became a coffin.

After he went to bed, I stopped on my way to get a drink of water and straightened my stiff, hunched shoulders. With my hand pressed to my breastbone, I drew a breath in.

Onni

I used to think of what it would be like if I'd had an older sister. An onni a hand's span taller than me. An onni to hand down slightly bobbled sweaters, patent leather shoes with only minor scuff marks.

An onni who would shrug on her coat and go to the pharmacy when our mother was ill. An onni who would put her finger to her lips and scold me: *quietly, you have to walk quietly.* An onni who could write out equations in my maths workbook. *This is really simple, you're just overthinking it.* Frowning as she hurried to reach the solution.

An onni who would tell me to sit down when I got a splinter in my foot. Who would bring the lamp over and, in its light, extract the splinter, ever so carefully, with a needle that she'd sterilised in the flame from the gas range.

An onni to come over when I'm huddled in the dark. *There's no need for that, it's all a misunderstanding.* A brief, awkward embrace. *Get up, for goodness' sake. Now let's eat.* A cold hand grazing my face. Her shoulders slipping swiftly away.

Like a clutch of words strewn over white paper

My black shoes stamped prints into the early-morning snow, a slushy layer sheeting the pavement.

Like a clutch of words strewn over white paper.

Seoul, which I had last seen in summer, had frozen.

Turning to look behind me, I saw the snow already sifting down to cover those just-made prints.

Whitening.

Mourning robes

Before two people get married, each gives clothes to the
other's parents. Silk clothes for those still living, cotton
mourning robes for the departed.

My brother called to check that I would go with him.
I waited until you came back, nuna.

The woman he was to marry had prepared a white
cotton skirt and jacket, which I spread out on the rock.
In a meadow of long grasses beneath the temple where
our mother's name is chanted after each morning's
sutras. As soon as I held my brother's lighter to the
sleeve, a thread of blue-tinged smoke spiralled up.
After white clothes dissolve into the air this way,
a spirit will wear them. Do we really believe that?

Smoke

We kept our eyes fixed intently on what was in front of
us, our mouths tightly shut. Smoke like a pair of ash-
grey wings was dissolving into the air. Disappearing.
I saw the fire, having consumed the jacket, run
instantly onto the skirt. When the last strip of cloth was
swallowed by the flames, I thought of you. If you can
come to us now, then do. Slip on those clothes that the
fire has borne to you, like slipping on a pair of a wings.
Drink it like medicine or tea, our silence, dissolving
into smoke in place of words.

Silence

When long days finally come to a close, a time to be
quiet is needed. As when, unconsciously in front of
a stove, I hold my stiff hands out to the silence, fingers
splayed in its scant warmth.

Lower teeth

The pronunciation of 'onni' resembles that of a baby's 'lower teeth'. Two tiny teeth like first leaves that had sprouted from my son's gums.

Now my son has grown up, and is no longer a baby. After pulling the quilt up to cover that twelve-year-old boy, I listened carefully for a while to his steady breathing, before returning to my empty desk.

Parting

Don't die. For God's sake don't die.

I open my lips and mutter the words you heard on opening your black eyes, you who were ignorant of language. I press down with all my strength onto the white paper. I believe that no better words of parting can be found. *Don't die. Live.*

All whiteness

With your eyes, I will see the deepest, most dazzling place within a white cabbage, the precious young petals concealed at its heart.

With your eyes, I will see the chill of the half-moon risen in the day.

At some point those eyes will see a glacier. They will look up at that enormous mass of ice and see something sacred, unsullied by life.

They will see inside the silence of the white birch forest. Inside the stillness of the window where the winter sun seeps in. Inside those shining grains of dust, swaying along the shafts of light which slant onto the ceiling.

Within that white, all of those white things, I will breathe in the final breath you released.